THE COLONIES

MODERN CURRICULUM PRESS

◎ Program Consultants

SHARON HARLEY, PH.D.
Associate Professor/Acting Director
African American Studies
University of Maryland

STEPHEN MIDDLETON, PH.D.
Assistant Professor of History
North Carolina University

◎ Program Reviewers

JACOB H. CARRUTHERS, PH.D.
Professor/Associate Director
Center For Inner City Studies
Northeastern Illinois University

BARBARA EMELLE, PH.D.
Associate Director of
Curriculum and Instruction
New Orleans Public Schools

PAUL HILL, JR.
Executive Director,
East End Neighborhood House
Cleveland, Ohio

SUBIRA KIFANO
Teacher Advisor
Language Development Program
  For African American Studies
Los Angeles Public Schools

MARY SHEPHERD LESTER
Director of Mathematics
Dallas Public Schools

LINDA LUPTON
Curriculum Coordinator
Cleveland Public Schools

GWENDOLYN MORRIS
Instructional Support Teacher
Philadelphia Public Schools

THOMASINA PORTIS
Director, Multicultural/Values Education
Washington, D.C. Public Schools

DOROTHY W. RILEY
Librarian and Author
Detroit, Michigan

Illustrators

Louis Pappas, Chapter Bottom Borders; Barbara Higgins Bond, 24, (bottom)28-29, 39; Mal Cann, 38 *(all three)*; Jennifer Hewitson, 17, 35; Ron Himler, 12, 21; Holly Jones, 14-15, 24, 25; Doug Knutson, 9 *(top)*, 30-31, 41; Al leiner, 27, 42; Dorothy Novick, 8-9 *(bottom)*, 20-21, 24 *(bottom)*; Pronto Design and Production, 10; Gary Thomas, 11, 23.

Photo Credits

American Antiquarian Society, 4-5, 24 *(bottom)*; The Bettmann Archive 13, 31; The Bostonian Society, 34; Colonial Williamsburg Foundation, 6-7; New York Public Library, 8-9 *(top)*,; Jack Couffer/Bruce Coleman, 32 *(bottom)*; Culver Pictures, 40; The Granger Collection, 22, 36-37, 38; Lois Greenfield/Bruce Coleman Inc., 32 *(middle center)*; The Great Blacks in Wax Museum, Inc., 15; Wolfgang Kaehler, Library of Congress, 26; 32 *(2nd from top)*; Lawrence Manning/Black Star, 32 *(top, middle left and right, 2nd from bottom)*; Rare Book Room, New York Public Library, 18-19; The North American Atlas, 33 *(top)*; Stokes Collection, New York Public Library, 20; From *Slavery and The Slave Trade–A Short Illustrated History*, By James Walvin, University Press of Mississippi, 33 (bottom).

Map Credits

Ortelius Design, 4, 16, 30, 32.

Acknowledgments

P. 16, Excerpt from *The African American Experience: A History*. Published by Globe Book Company, Inc.© 1992.
P. 38, Art by Mal Cann based on art by Susan Willmath in *Black History for Beginners*, Writers and Readers Publishing, Inc., 1984.
Every reasonable effort has been made to locate the ownership of copyrighted materials and to make due acknowledgment. Any errors or omissions will be gladly rectified in future editions.

Design & Production: TWINC, Catherine Wahl, Kurt Kaptur
Executive Editor: Marty Nordquist
Project Editor: June M. Howland

MODERN CURRICULUM PRESS
13900 Prospect Road, Cleveland, Ohio 44136
Simon & Schuster • A Paramount Communications Company

Based on *The African American Experience: A History* published by Globe Book Company © 1992.

ISBN 0-8136-4959-5 (Reinforced Binding)   ISBN 0-8136-4960-9 (Paperback)

10 9 8 7 6 5 4 3 2   97 96 95 94

CONTENTS

HISTORY SPEAKS 5
CHAPTER 1 6
   Africans in the Southern Colonies 7
   The Growth of Slavery 10
   A Short Freedom 11
   Plantation Life 12
   Unfair Controls 14
   Talk About It • Write About It 17
CHAPTER 2 18
   Africans in the Middle Colonies 19
   Many Kinds of Work 20
   The Question of Slavery 22
   The Other Middle Colonies 24
   Talk About It • Write About It 27
CHAPTER 3 28
   Africans in the New England Colonies 29
   The Heart of the Slave Trade 30
   A Better Life 33
   Talk About It • Write About It 35
CHAPTER 4 36
   Seeking Freedom 37
   Rising Up for Freedom 40
   Talk About It • Write About It 42
ECHOES 43
TIMELINE 44
GLOSSARY 46
INDEX 48

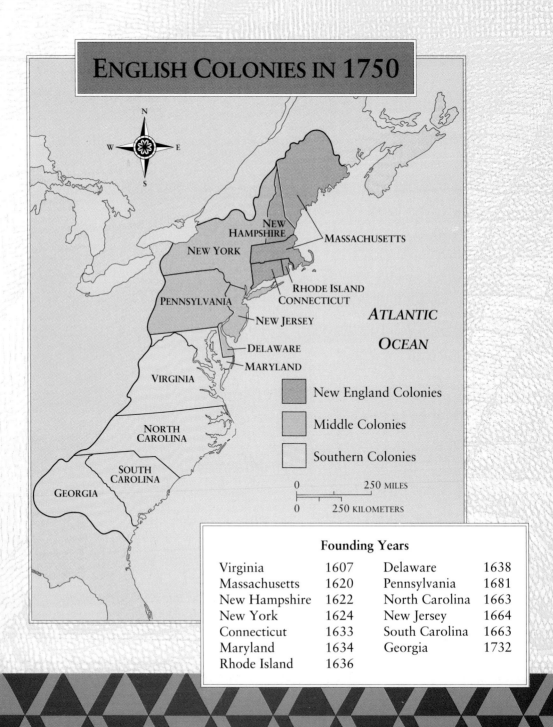

ENGLISH COLONIES IN 1750

New England Colonies

Middle Colonies

Southern Colonies

0   250 MILES

0   250 KILOMETERS

ATLANTIC OCEAN

NEW HAMPSHIRE
MASSACHUSETTS
NEW YORK
RHODE ISLAND
CONNECTICUT
PENNSYLVANIA
NEW JERSEY
DELAWARE
MARYLAND
VIRGINIA
NORTH CAROLINA
SOUTH CAROLINA
GEORGIA

Founding Years

Virginia	1607	Delaware	1638
Massachusetts	1620	Pennsylvania	1681
New Hampshire	1622	North Carolina	1663
New York	1624	New Jersey	1664
Connecticut	1633	South Carolina	1663
Maryland	1634	Georgia	1732
Rhode Island	1636		

HISTORY
SPEAKS

The enslavement of Africans during colonial times marks the beginning of a tragic chapter in America's history. Taking root in Jamestown by 1660, slavery spread throughout the colonies. By the mid-1700s, each of the English colonies had adopted slavery. Although Africans were treated differently from place to place, most were bought and sold like merchandise in a store. The free labor of enslaved Africans helped many European settlers to become wealthy and established, and many African workers to become poor and excluded.

No matter in which colony they lived, or what kind of work they did, enslaved Africans fought against bondage in any way they could. Their requests for freedom were not heard by most colonists, even though a few believed slavery was wrong. In spite of slavery, the rich ancestry of Africans has become a part of American heritage. ✹

1

In 1619 twenty Africans were brought to Jamestown, the first colony to succeed in America. This important event would forever change the history of two continents — Africa and North America. These Africans worked as servants for a number of years and then were freed. Later, most Africans brought to the Southern colonies of Virginia, Maryland, Georgia, North Carolina, and South Carolina were forced to serve as slaves for life. ❀

Arival of the first Africans brought to Jamestown.

AFRICANS IN THE SOUTHERN COLONIES

Chained with other captured Africans, Antoney and Isabella wondered what was going to happen to them. Packed below the deck in a hot, dirty cargo hold, they had survived a terrible journey across the Atlantic Ocean. First they had been taken from their villages in Africa by Spanish traders planning to sell them in the West Indies. Then during the crossing, they had been stolen from the Spanish by Dutch pirates. Forced aboard a Dutch ship, they were brought to the English settlement at Jamestown, Virginia, in 1619. There they were finally traded for food.

Founded in 1607, the colony of Jamestown was just beginning to develop when the first Africans arrived. After English settlers had spent years living in a wilderness, battling disease, and learning how to raise new crops, their colony was starting to expand. This was due to the increasing demand for tobacco in Europe. Growing tobacco, which became the colony's main crop, created a huge demand for workers. New settlers soon flocked to this area.

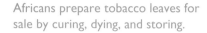
Africans prepare tobacco leaves for sale by curing, dying, and storing.

The Southern colonies of America were settled from 1607 to 1732. Virginia was the first colony to use Africans as workers. Because tobacco crops wore the land out quickly, planters were always moving on to new lands. The new lands had to be cleared, so more workers were always needed.

There were not enough colonists to do all the work necessary to keep up with the demand for tobacco. So during the early 1600s, the people of Jamestown used *indentured servants* to work the land. New settlers were offered a bonus of fifty acres of land for each indentured servant they brought with them. Many European settlers indentured themselves as servants to pay for their passage to the Americas.

When Antoney and Isabella—part of an unexpected cargo—arrived in Jamestown, they too were sold as indentured servants. They and the other

Early Jamestown, the first colony settled on the continent North America.

Africans would work for at least seven years before they were released. When their contracts were completed, they would be free to buy land and become colonial settlers. Becoming settlers possibly meant they could vote and would be protected by the laws of the colony.

A few years after their arrival, Antoney and Isabella were allowed to marry. In 1624, they had a son they named William. He was the first African born in all of the colonies. William was born free, but future generations of Africans would be born slaves.

From 1619 through the 1660s, most African arrivals to the Southern colonies were indentured servants rather than slaves. They worked side by side with many Native Americans and European indentured servants. African and European servants both arrived in the colonies facing a future of hard work before they would be free to live their own lives. The use of indentured servants helped the colonies grow.

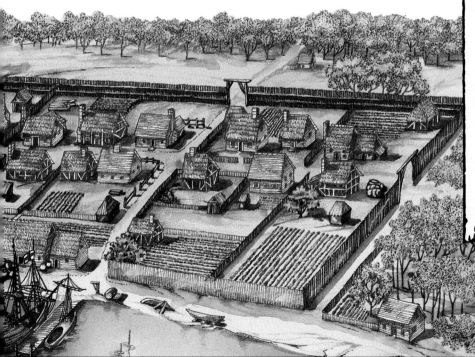

The Growth of Slavery

In the Southern colonies not all indentured servants were treated equally. Africans were early targets for *discrimination.* Africans were different in appearance and habits, and they were not *Christians* as were most of the European settlers. Because of these differences, many Southern colonists looked down on Africans and did not treat them the same as other people.

Southern Colonies began separating European indentured servants from African indentured servants. They created strict rules that applied only to Africans. The Southern colonists took more and more control of the Africans' lives.

By the late-1600s, enslaved Africans were replacing indentured servants as the main workers in the Southern colonies. There were many reasons for this. Not enough Europeans were willing to come to the colonies as indentured servants, but more workers were needed. Also, indentured servants cost more to keep as workers than slaves. Slaves were often given less food, clothing, and shelter than indentured servants. Finally, Africans who could be enslaved to work for life were of more value to owners than servants who only worked for a limited period of time.

What conclusions about American colonists can you draw by comparing these graphs?

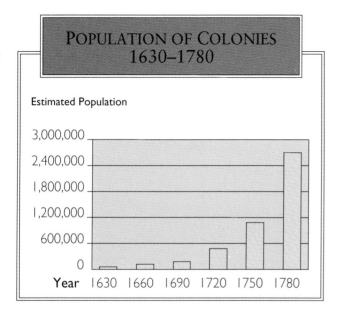

POPULATION OF COLONIES 1630–1780

Estimated Population

3,000,000	
2,400,000	
1,800,000	
1,200,000	
600,000	
0	

Year   1630   1660   1690   1720   1750   1780

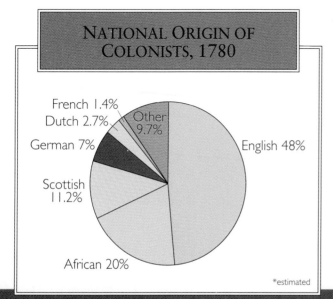

NATIONAL ORIGIN OF COLONISTS, 1780

French 1.4%
Dutch 2.7%
Other 9.7%
German 7%
English 48%
Scottish 11.2%
African 20%

*estimated

A Short Freedom

Although most Africans in the Southern colonies were slaves, there were a few who were free. By 1651, Anthony Johnson and his wife Mary were finally working for themselves. They stood with pride as they gazed out on the 250 acres of land that they now owned. Indentured as servants thirty years before, the Johnsons had saved their money and purchased land after completing their contracts.

Working nearby in half-cleared fields were five indentured servants. Some were African and some were European, and all were indentured to Anthony and Mary.

This would be the beginning of a real home for the Johnson children even though they realized they and their parents were unwilling *immigrants*. In the following years, one of the children acquired more land and named the *plantation* "Angola," perhaps in memory of the African homeland of Anthony's family.

Other free Africans settled near Angola. The Johnsons and this small group of neighbors formed the first free African community in America. Opportunities for Africans to have this much freedom would not last long. As more and more Africans came to the English colonies, the security of their freedom became weaker.

Plantation Life

While slavery would eventually exist in all the colonies, it was most widespread in the South. These colonies grew and prospered through farming. The *geography* and climate of this region made it possible for crops to be grown all year round.

Southern colonists found markets in England for their tobacco as well as rice, *indigo*, and sugar cane. To meet the huge demand for these crops, planters grew them on plantations.

Many workers were needed to tend the plantation lands, but planters wanted to spend as little money as possible. To fill the need for cheap labor, they bought Africans to use as slaves. This desire for cheap labor helped slavery grow.

Most enslaved Africans in the South worked as field hands or outdoor farm workers. Some became house servants. A few were trained as skilled workers—carpenters, shoemakers, blacksmiths, barrel makers, and leather workers. Most enslaved Africans lived in separate "slave" quarters away from the owner's house. Their tiny, bare shacks might have contained a couple of benches, a table, and a frying pan. Many shacks had only straw on a dirt floor. Some Africans were allowed to keep small gardens.

At auctions like this one, African family members were sometimes sold apart.

However, work on the plantations left them little time to tend their own gardens or to be with their families.

Sometimes African families were cruelly torn apart and family members were sold to different owners. Southern land owners usually did not respect African marriages. Time and time again husbands were sold away from wives, and children were sold away from parents. One Southern slave recalled a horrible memory of being torn from his mother:

> My new master took me before him . . . and started home; but my poor mother, when she saw me leaving her for the last time, ran after me. . . . My mother . . . cried, 'Oh, master, do not take me from my child!' Without making a reply, he gave her two or three heavy blows on the shoulders with his rawhide, . . . and . . . dragged her back toward the place of sale.

Unfair Controls

Southern plantation owners tried to destroy Africans' ties to their homeland in order to keep them enslaved. Planters forbade Africans to make drums, which would allow them to communicate with each other as they did in their native land. They even kept Africans who spoke the same language apart. Owners did not allow Africans to worship in the religious ways of their ancestors. They forced many to become Christians and to use English names.

Africans were not allowed to travel freely. They could not leave their plantation home without permission from the owners. They were not allowed to go to school or to learn to read and write English. Planters did not care that some Africans were well-educated and could already read and write in their native languages.

In spite of all these restrictions, the stories of their native land did not disappear. Africans passed their history and important stories down by word of mouth whenever they could. Dates of birth, names of ancestors, and memories of their homeland were just a few of the things that they memorized and shared. From generation to generation their history lived on.

During the 1600s, the number of Africans in the Southern

Modern-day griot, Mary Carter Smith, and her husband pose with her wax figure in a Maryland museum.

colonies was fairly small, but growing steadily. By the early 1700s, Africans made up nearly half the people in the Southern colonies. In South Carolina there were more Africans than colonists.

THE GRIOT SPEAKS

Please sit down and join me as I tell you my story. I am a *griot* (gree-OH) of West Africa. I am the keeper of my people's history and a teller of stories. From one generation to another, griots pass along all we have seen and heard. Can I tell you interesting things of the people and places of Africa? Why yes! Will I make you laugh, stare in surprise, or maybe even cry with my tales? Perhaps. Sit with me awhile and listen . . . .

The tradition of the griot is as ancient as Africa itself. A griot is a historian and an educator. Some Africans brought to the colonies were griots and many were forced to act as griots because of restrictions placed on them from slave owners. By telling and retelling their history and stories of Africa, these masters of the spoken word preserved their culture.

Alex Haley, the author of *Roots*, was determined to find out exactly who his ancestors were and where they came from. A long trail finally led him to a griot in Gambia, West Africa. The griot was able to recite to him the entire history of his ancestors from which a book and a movie were made.

Concerned about the growing number of Africans, plantation owners created strict laws to keep them *captive*. These laws were called *slave codes*. Under these codes enslaved Africans had to be inside by a certain time of night. They were not allowed to gather with other Africans. Anyone caught breaking these rules was punished harshly. Slaves guilty of other crimes, such as trying to escape or raising a revolt, were sometimes put to death. Punishments were often given to Africans simply to show owners' control. "Once they whipped my father 'cause he looked at a slave they killed and cried," said Roberta Mason.

For many years to come, most Africans in the South would live under harsh and brutal conditions. In 1650, there were only three hundred Africans in Virginia. By 1750, the number jumped to 120,000 out of a *population* of 293,000. These numbers continued to rise as more and more Africans were brought to the Americas.

AFRICAN AMERICAN POPULATION OF SOUTHERN COLONIES, 1750

DELAWARE

VIRGINIA

MARYLAND

APPALACHIAN MOUNTAINS

NORTH CAROLINA

▲ = 1,000 people

SOUTH CAROLINA

ATLANTIC OCEAN

GEORGIA

0   250 MILES

0   250 KILOMETERS

TALK ABOUT IT

◎ Do you think the enslavement of Africans for life was fair or unfair? How are some groups of people treated unfairly today? Why does this happen?

◎ What do you think was the most difficult thing for an enslaved African child to endure? Explain your answer.

◎ Africans passed history, stories, and other information down to younger people by word of mouth. Why? What things have you learned this way? From whom have you learned them?

WRITE ABOUT IT

You are a newspaper reporter in Virginia in the 1600s. You are asked to write a story about what a typical week in the life of a plantation slave is like. To do this you will have to research the facts. Then write your story.

2

By the 1640s the practice of enslaving Africans was quickly spreading throughout the Middle colonies of New York, New Jersey, Delaware, and Pennsylvania. They were called the Middle colonies because they were located between the Southern and the New England colonies. More Africans in these colonies had a chance for freedom, but many were enslaved for life. ✳

Europeans settled the first Middle colony, New Amsterdam, later called New York, in 1624.

rd exc. cum Priv. ord. Holl. et Westfr.

AFRICANS IN THE MIDDLE COLONIES

The Middle colonies of America were settled from 1624 to 1681. Africans were among the first settlers, but did not come to the Middle colonies as free people. Some arrived by slave ship, having been captured from their homeland. Some were traded to Middle colonists by Southern plantation owners. Others arrived as indentured servants of European settlers.

European settlers also came to America for different reasons. Dutch merchants seeking animal furs to trade settled in New York, or New Amsterdam as it was first called. German, Scottish, and Irish people came looking for a fresh start in life. Also, there were those who came to the Middle colonies looking for religious freedom—**Quakers**, French Protestants, Jews, and Catholics.

Slavery did not take root as deeply in the Middle colonies as it had in the Southern colonies. There were many different people in this area with varied opinions about the enslavement of Africans. Many felt it was wrong to own another human.

PETER WILLIAMS

What was life like for enslaved Africans in the Middle colonies?

Peter Williams led a life common to many enslaved Africans.

He was bought and sold many times. Peter Williams' third owner, a tobacco merchant, sold him to the officers of the colonists' Episcopal Church. He rang the bell for the church services, took care of the building, and dug graves for those who were buried there.

Williams borrowed money from friends and bought his freedom. He went on working at the Episcopal Church until the end of his life.

Many Kinds of Work

Africans in the Middle colonies often worked alongside their owners. Often they lived with their owners—either in back rooms, attics, or small buildings near the house.

Despite this, most Africans in the Middle colonies had little hope of freedom. However, they were not controlled by laws as harsh as those in the South. This was because slaves were not as important to the growth of these colonies' economy as in the South.

Most of the farms in the Middle colonies were much smaller than the plantations in the South and needed fewer workers. The region's climate did not suit a plantation system. It was much colder in the Middle colonies than in the Southern colonies, and farms could not be worked all year round. Most farmers could not afford to keep enslaved Africans in the winter when fields were not being worked.

Farming brought many settlers a good living, however. Crops of rye and wheat were plentiful enough to sell in America and Europe. Some industry also grew out of these farming efforts. Wheat was turned into flour at mills. The beginnings of an iron industry developed and many Africans worked in skilled trades in the Middle colonies. For example, Peter Williams became a cigar maker for his owner, a tobacco merchant.

"Do I hear $74? Do I hear $100? Going once. Going twice. . . Sold to the man in the suit! . . ."

Sales of captive Africans in the Middle colonies were advertised everywhere. Most Africans were purchased through *auctions*. An auction is a public sale in which the highest bidder buys the merchandise.

On sale day planters, *overseers,* and other buyers, looked over the Africans, examining teeth, eyes, skin, and bone structure. The captives were then auctioned off "by the candle." This meant that those who wanted to buy an African could bid until one inch of candle had burned down.

If any Africans were left at the end of the auction, they were sold by "scramble." All buyers would rush and grab the Africans they wanted. Sometimes, slave auctions lasted for days.

The Question of Slavery

Of all the Middle colonies, it was in New York that the question of whether or not to have slavery would be most difficult to answer. Two different attitudes about slavery existed in this colony.

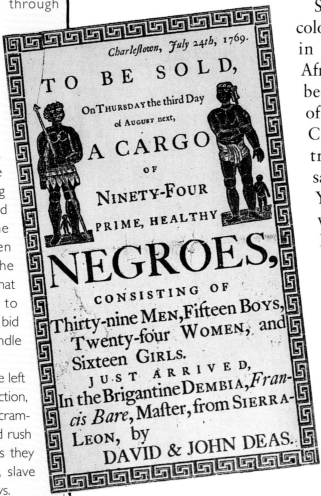

Charlestown, July 24th, 1769.

TO BE SOLD, On THURSDAY the third Day of AUGUST next, A CARGO OF NINETY-FOUR PRIME, HEALTHY NEGROES, CONSISTING OF Thirty-nine MEN, Fifteen Boys, Twenty-four WOMEN, and Sixteen GIRLS. JUST ARRIVED, In the Brigantine DEMBIA, Francis Bare, Master, from SIERRA-LEON, by DAVID & JOHN DEAS.

Some New York colonists strongly believed in enslavement of Africans. The colony had been founded by agents of the Dutch West India Company in 1623. Its traders brought thousands of slaves to New York. By 1640 there were more Africans in New York than in any of the Middle colonies.

Then there were those colonists who were against enslavement of Africans in New York. It had been the first of all the colonies to respect freedom of religion. As a result, people of different religions had come to this colony. These settlers usually did not believe in the enslavement of others.

After much *debate*, laws were passed that allowed for the enslavement of Africans, but only in certain situations. Enslaved and indentured servants could also turn to the courts for help if they thought their rights had been ignored. By the mid-1700s, there were as many as

11,000 Africans out of a total population of 75,000 living in the colony of New York.

In 1644, Simon Congo, Anthony Portuguese, and nine African Americans stood breathless before the Council of New Netherlands (New York). They had *petitioned* for their freedom and now were waiting to hear the council's decision. Eighteen years before, as indentured servants, they had helped the Dutch build the village of New Amsterdam, that was now New York. In return, they had been promised their freedom by agents of the Dutch West India Company. The huge slave-trading company, however, had not kept its promise.

The fate of Congo, Portuguese, and the other servants was finally decided. The Council of New Netherlands had finally ruled that the eleven men should be freed from their bondage. The council gave each of them a piece of land and the same rights as any other Dutch citizen. This meant these men could now trade, vote, own land, and testify in court against other colonists.

The Other Middle Colonies

Slavery was not as deeply rooted in Pennsylvania as in New York. This colony had been founded in 1681 by William Penn as a place for Quakers and others to practice their religion freely. The Quakers had been told they were not welcome in England or other colonies. After settling in Pennsylvania they vowed to practice their beliefs as they saw fit.

They were against war and violence, and believed they should offer kindness and help to all people. They knew what it was like to be treated differently than others. Most had sympathy for the position of enslaved Africans who had been brought to America against their will. However, some did not.

A small number of Quakers did hold Africans in bondage. They reasoned that if the Africans were treated kindly and had not been sold against their will it was all right to keep them as servants. Many of the servants never received their freedom, however. Quakers also felt that it was their duty to teach Africans about Christianity, which could be done if Africans were enslaved.

Trouble often broke out between Quakers who did not hold slaves and those who did. Benjamin Lay was one Quaker who did not believe in keeping slaves.

It was the middle of winter in 1745. Benjamin Lay shivered as he stood barefoot in the snow. The crowd of Quakers leaving the meeting stared at him. He acted as if nothing was wrong or unusual. Finally a passerby told him he was in danger of catching cold.

Benjamin pointed out that the Quakers' slaves were in the same condition as he—lacking shelter and proper clothing. He asked them how they could worry about him and yet not worry about their slaves.

Benjamin knew firsthand what it was like to be treated unfairly. Many people excluded him from Quaker meetings because he was different from others. He was only four feet seven inches tall and had a hunchback, a huge head, and a full beard. Since Benjamin was familiar with discrimination, Benjamin did everything he could to convince those Quakers who owned Africans to free them.

Slavery grew slower in the Middle colony of Pennsylvania than in any of the other colonies. By the 1750s, the small population of enslaved Africans there had gained more rights than Africans in any other colony.

Africans in Delaware had the least freedom of all those in the Middle colonies. This colony's climate made tobacco production on plantations profitable. Although Delaware had also been settled by Quakers in 1682, this colony was closely linked to Southern slave-holding colonies. Settlers in Delaware bought Africans to work the plantations and created laws to make it difficult for Africans to gain freedom. ✳

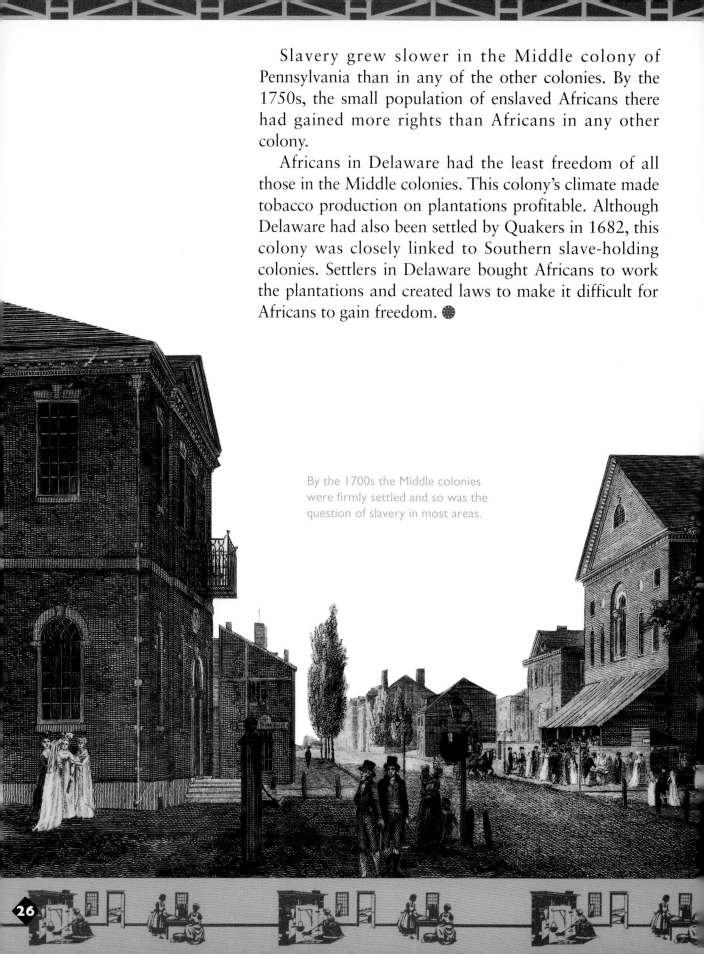

By the 1700s the Middle colonies were firmly settled and so was the question of slavery in most areas.

TALK ABOUT IT

◎ **What do you think were the greatest contributions Africans made to the Middle colonies?**

◎ **If you were an escaped African, would you be better off running away to New York, Pennsylvania, or Delaware? Why?**

◎ **Do you think the lives of enslaved Africans in the Middle colonies were better, worse, or the same as those that lived in the Southern colonies? Why?**

WRITE ABOUT IT

You are a Quaker who buys a tobacco plantation in Delaware. You are leaning towards buying enslaved Africans as workers. Your neighbor is Benjamin Lay, who does not think owning slaves is right. What arguments would each of you use to support your opinions? Write a few statements you might use to explain your idea of owning slaves. Then, write a few arguments Benjamin Lay might use to talk you out of it.

3

In the 1600s and 1700s, New England was the center of the slave trade. Although most of the settlers in the colonies of Massachusetts, Rhode Island, New Hampshire, and Connecticut did not own slaves themselves, they helped slave trading to continue and expand.

This child , Phillis Wheatley, and many other Africans were brought to America and sold as slaves.

Africans in the New England Colonies

In July, 1761, John Avery, an agent for slave ship captains, looked over his cargo. Those Africans who had lived through the trip across the Atlantic Ocean had been fed and rubbed with oil to make them look healthy. Susannah Wheatley, a wealthy Massachusetts woman, needed a servant to work in her home. She had just seen an advertisement announcing the arrival of a cargo of slaves which read,

> "A Parcel of likely Negroes, imported from Africa, cheap for cash . . . . Enquire of John Avery . . . ."

Mrs. Wheatley went to the slave market near the shore of the bay in Boston, Massachusetts. She saw a thin, sickly African girl of about eight years old. Shivering with cold, Phillis had no clothing other than a dirty carpet wrapped around her. Phillis stood there silent, hanging her head as she was looked over from head to toe. Susannah decided at once to buy her. John Avery charged only a small sum for the girl because he thought she was going to die.

Although the use of slaves was not widespread in the New England colonies through the 1600s and 1700s, it was legal. This area was the very heart of the slave trade in America.

Most New England colonists did not use Africans as workers, but sold them to make money. They sold thousands upon thousands of Africans to the Middle and especially the Southern colonies. The trade was important to the area's economy. As late as 1735, there were only 2,600 Africans in the New England colonies out of a population of 141,000.

The Heart of the Slave Trade

The thin, rocky soil and cooler climate of New England made farming difficult. The area had some small farms but no plantations and no need for large numbers of workers. Because farming was difficult, many settlers turned to the sea to make a living. The New England *economy* grew from fishing and trading. Soon, the slave trading industry became the foundation of the economy.

By 1698 a *triangular trade* was underway. A ship would take a cargo of rum from New England to Africa, where the captain would use it to buy captured Africans. An average New England trading ship could hold about seventy-five Africans. The Africans were then taken to the West Indies where they were sold. There the captain bought sugar and molasses which he took back to New England to be sold. By the end of this trading process most ship captains made a huge profit.

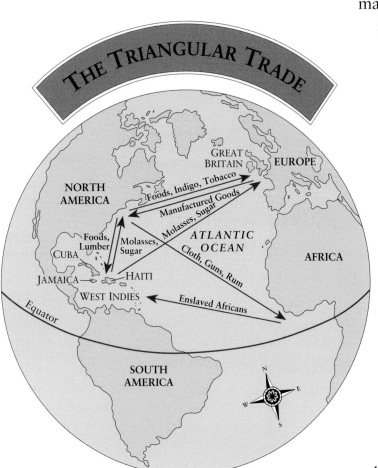

Because of the New England slave trade, the number of Africans in the thirteen colonies grew from 59,000 in 1714, to 300,000 in 1754. Slave dealers made so much money that enslaved Africans came to be called *black gold*.

Cargos of Africans like this one came to New England ports daily.

Many of the leaders in the slave trade were *Puritans.* These were English people who were unhappy with the Church of England. They had come to Massachusetts in 1620 to find a safe place to worship. They also wanted to set up a model Christian community.

The Puritans had to decide whether or not to allow slavery in their colony. It was a difficult question. How could they be Christians and keep people enslaved? After much debate, in 1641 the Puritans made slavery legal in Massachusetts under certain circumstances. Slavery was allowed if the enslaved persons were captured in a war or were sold to the Puritans by traders. The Puritans had come to a new land looking for freedom. It turned out they took the freedom of many Africans.

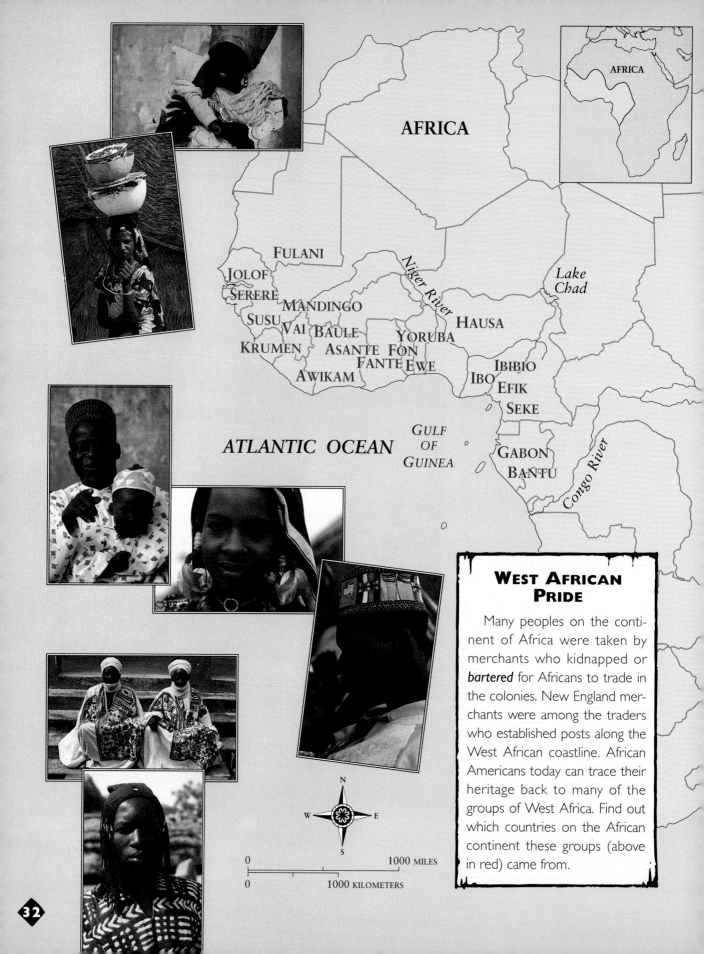

AFRICA

FULANI

JOLOF
SERERE
MANDINGO
SUSU
VAI BAULE
KRUMEN ASANTE FON
FANTE EWE
AWIKAM

Niger River

HAUSA

YORUBA

*Lake
Chad*

IBIBIO
IBO EFIK
SEKE

ATLANTIC OCEAN

GULF
OF
GUINEA

GABON
BANTU

Congo River

AFRICA

N
W — E
S

0 ——————— 1000 MILES
0 ——————— 1000 KILOMETERS

WEST AFRICAN PRIDE

Many peoples on the continent of Africa were taken by merchants who kidnapped or *bartered* for Africans to trade in the colonies. New England merchants were among the traders who established posts along the West African coastline. African Americans today can trace their heritage back to many of the groups of West Africa. Find out which countries on the African continent these groups (above in red) came from.

32

Africans and European colonists often worked together on shipping docks in the New England colonies.

A Better Life

The Puritans in the New England colonies treated enslaved Africans as human beings, not property. They gave Africans some rights. Most Africans in New England had more schooling than those in the other colonies and learned to read and write. This was because the Puritans wanted captive Africans to read the Bible and become Christians.

In New England enslaved Africans could own property and had the right to a trial by a jury. They could defend their rights in court and testify against colonists in legal cases. Slave codes were not very harsh and were rarely enforced. Few crimes were punished by death, and owners did not have the power of life or death over those they held as slaves.

Many Africans in the New England colonies received formal burials often attended by their owners.

PHILLIS WHEATLEY, POET

Should you, my lord, while you peruse my song,

Wonder from when my love of Freedom sprung,

Whence flow these wishes for the common good,

By feeling hearts alone best understood,

I, young in life, by seeming cruel fate

Was snatched from Africa's fancied happy seat . . .

If Phillis were alive today, she might say this same thing like this:

If you wonder where I got my love for freedom
and for everyone,

It is because when I was young I was taken from my home.

Phillis Wheatley became a house servant for the Wheatley family. Many enslaved Africans in New England were treated as part of the family and lived in the same house as their owners. Few Africans worked as field hands. Many worked on New England's docks or on ships as deck hands or cooks. Others worked as skilled crafts workers, such as printers, carpenters, or iron workers.

She learned to read from the Bible and was given lessons in Latin, history, and geography. She proved to have a great talent in writing. By the time she was fifteen years old, Phillis had written a poem to the King of England. Two years later a collection of her poetry was published in America and then in England. Phillis became the first African American to have a book published in the colonies and the second woman to do so. ✸

TALK ABOUT IT

◎ Why do you think the New England colonists were more willing than the Southern colonists to work side by side with enslaved Africans?

◎ What do you think would have been different in the American colonies if people in New England had not gotten involved in the slave trade?

◎ Compare how Phillis Wheatley might have felt on two important days of her life: when she was bought by Mrs. Wheatley and the day her book was published.

WRITE ABOUT IT

Phillis Wheatley wrote many poems about her life in Massachusetts and Africa. Many people have read her poems and written detailed information about her life. Find out more information about her. Write a summary of the interesting things you find to share with your friends.

4

In all of colonial America, an unequal treatment of Africans existed. Whether enslaved or free, none of them were given the same rights as European colonists. Although the expansion of the colonies increased the debate over the unfairness of slavery, the horrible conditions continued. Africans dreamed, planned, worked, and died for freedom. ✸

Nat Turner tells other African Americans about his plan to lead them to freedom.

Seeking Freedom

Africans did not easily submit to the brutal treatment they received as slaves. They tried any way they could to gain freedom. During the voyage across the Atlantic Ocean, some used their chains as weapons, took over ships, and tried to return to Africa. One sailor wrote, "If care not be taken they will *mutiny* and destroy the ship's crew." Between 1699 and 1845 ship diaries document fifty-five African *uprisings* aboard ships.

Many captives aboard slave ships tried to kill themselves. They would not eat, or jumped into the ocean. Many showed that they would rather die than live in captivity.

Once enslaved to colonial settlers, many Africans continued their efforts to gain freedom. Some successfully escaped from their owners. A few Africans found safety with nearby Native Americans. Many advertisements for escaped slaves filled colonial newspapers.

AFRICANS AND NATIVE AMERICANS

Do you think it was surprising that Africans and Native Americans met and helped each other? The Europeans took the Native Americans' land and made the Africans work it.

When Native Americans tried to defend their land, they fought against colonists and spared most Africans. People from the two groups also married and had children. The following is an advertisement for escaped slaves that shows the bond:

Runaway on the 20th of September last, from Silas Pavin . . . in New Jersey, a very lusty Negro fellow named Sampson, aged about 53 years, and had some Indian blood in him. . . . He had with him a boy of about 12 or 13 years of age named Sam, was born of an Indian woman, and looks like an Indian. . . . They are both well clothed, only the boy is barefooted. . . . They both talk Indian very well, and it is likely they have dressed themselves in the Indian dress, and gone to Carolina.

Many Africans and Native Americans like the Seminoles worked together against slavery. The name Seminole means runaways.

Osecola, a Seminole chief.

Abraham, an African interpreter.

Caocoochee, a friend to escaped slaves.

A number of Africans were set free by their owners, as a reward for special services. Others earned enough money to buy their freedom. One free man even became an indentured servant so he could buy the freedom of his wife who was enslaved. It was common for free family members to seek their relations who were still enslaved. This spirit of family would help take Africans a long way in their struggles for equality and freedom.

Once colonial laws had been established, some enslaved Africans even took their owners to court to gain their freedom. In 1769 a slave in New England named James brought charges against his owner, claiming he had "restrained him of his liberty and held him

TEN DOLLARS REWARD.

RAN away, on the 23d inft. a handfome active *Mulatto* flave, named ARCH, about 21 years of age, is flender built and of middle ftature, talks fenfible and artful, but if clofly examined is apt to tremble, has a ridge or fcar on

Ads like this often ran in colonial newspapers.

in servitude." When James lost the case, he took it to a higher court and won.

Africans brought many skills from their homeland and greatly contributed to the prosperity of the American colonies. They were much more familiar with the environment of the colonies than the English settlers. Africans were not only farmers, but they were builders, and caregivers for many of the slave owners.

Many Africans had great knowledge of a strong planting system that

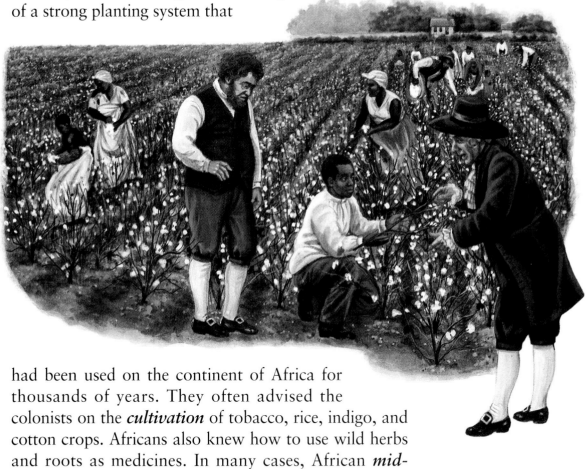

had been used on the continent of Africa for thousands of years. They often advised the colonists on the *cultivation* of tobacco, rice, indigo, and cotton crops. Africans also knew how to use wild herbs and roots as medicines. In many cases, African *midwives* who helped during childbirth were more respected than colonial doctors.

Slave owners were dependent on Africans to manage many parts of colonial life. Often proving themselves equal to their white owners, it became more and more difficult for Africans to remain enslaved without hope of being freed.

Many Africans escaped in the night like these traveling along the Stono River. Why do you think travel at night was necessary?

Rising Up for Freedom

As their hardships worsened under the restrictions of bondage, many Africans began to rise up in *rebellion.* Most of the *uprisings* were put down, but captive Africans still risked everything—torture and even death—to make a stand for freedom. As the number of Africans grew in the colonies, colonists in both the North and South feared African rebellions more and more. Colonists passed harsher slave codes as a way of maintaining control.

Uprisings by enslaved Africans began in the colonies as early as 1658. Africans were sometimes joined by Native Americans in these rebellions. In 1739, a group of escaped Africans built a fort near St. Augustine, Florida, to protect their families from slave catchers. The Spanish who lived there helped the Africans because the English and Spanish were enemies. The Seminole Indians also aided them.

On September 9, 1739, a group of escaped Africans gathered outside of Charleston, South Carolina, and started out to join those at the fort. Unlike most escaping Africans, they did not run or hide. Their shouts for liberty filled the air as they marched boldly with homemade flags flying along the Stono River. Armed with stolen weapons, they had risen up against their owners and made a break for freedom.

As they moved south, black smoke from plantations they had burned filled the sky behind them. At one point, unaware that they were surrounded by colonial soldiers, they stopped to rest. Filled with triumph and thoughts of freedom, they began dancing and singing in the fields. Suddenly, the soldiers opened fire. Some Africans escaped, but many were caught and killed. This rebellion, known as the Stono Uprising, was not the end of the African fight for freedom. The next two hundred years would show that the stand for equal rights taken by these first Africans in America had set a pattern. From that time forward, through faith and constant effort, African Americans would eventually be free. ✹

RESISTANCE ACROSS THE COLONIES

1658
Enslaved Africans and Native Americans join together and burn owners' homes in Hartford, Connecticut.

1663
African slaves plot to rise up against owners in Gloucester County, Virginia, but they are discovered.

1708
Two slaves, an African and a Native American, kill their owner's family on Long Island, New York.

1739
Slaves rise up near the Stono River.

1741
New York colonists blame Africans for a wave of fires and thefts. They refer to the incident as the "Great Negro Plot."

1800
An African American slave in Virginia named Gabriel Prosser planned to lead fellow Africans to freedom as Moses led the Israelites out of Egypt. His well-thought-out plan failed.

1831
Nat Turner leads a rebellion.

TALK ABOUT IT

◎ Why do you think enslaved Africans often ran away to Native American settlements? What do you think Africans and Native Americans had in common with each other?

◎ Why do you think it was possible for the colonists, who themselves wanted freedom from Great Britain, to take away the freedom of enslaved Africans?

◎ How might the United States be different today if slavery had never been allowed in the colonies?

WRITE ABOUT IT

Think about what living in the Southern colonies in 1739 was like. Read more about the colonies to find out. Then take the role of either an enslaved African or a slave owner who has just read in the newspaper about an uprising of enslaved Africans. Write a letter to the editor expressing how you feel about this event.

ECHOES
FROM THE COLONIES

Taken from their homeland and brought across the Atlantic Ocean in chains, Africans were forced into slavery and helped the Europeans build a permanent home on the continent of North America. From the plantations of the South to the shipyards of New England, the skill and strength of Africans became the cornerstone of the colonial settlements.

How would you react if you were taken from your home—from your parents and your friends—forever? What if you were brought to a strange country and forced to work for someone else, with no hope of ever being free? What feelings would you have?

By the 1700s there were basically two separate populations in the colonies—one European and free, one African and enslaved. The story of Africans in America is the story of a brave people who fought to help build America, even though they were not free to enjoy the benefits of this new country. What can you learn from these Africans?

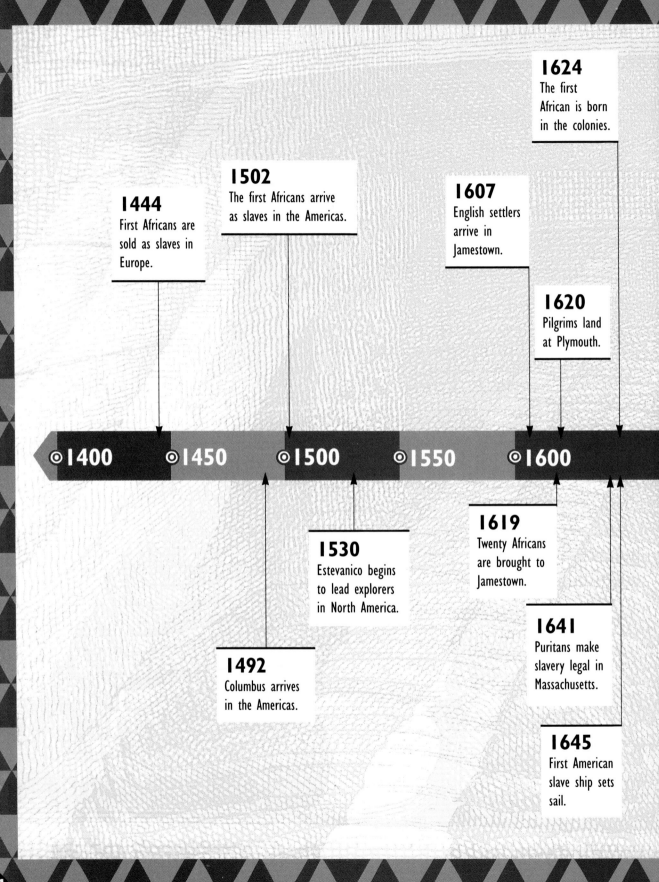

1624
The first African is born in the colonies.

1502
The first Africans arrive as slaves in the Americas.

1607
English settlers arrive in Jamestown.

1444
First Africans are sold as slaves in Europe.

1620
Pilgrims land at Plymouth.

◉1400   ◉1450   ◉1500   ◉1550   ◉1600

1530
Estevanico begins to lead explorers in North America.

1619
Twenty Africans are brought to Jamestown.

1641
Puritans make slavery legal in Massachusetts.

1492
Columbus arrives in the Americas.

1645
First American slave ship sets sail.

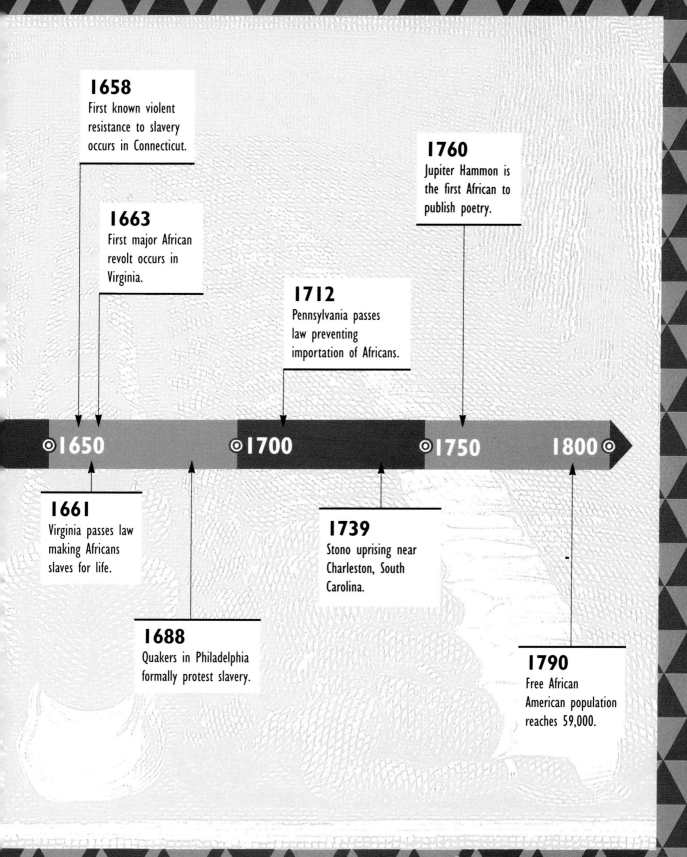

1658
First known violent resistance to slavery occurs in Connecticut.

1663
First major African revolt occurs in Virginia.

1760
Jupiter Hammon is the first African to publish poetry.

1712
Pennsylvania passes law preventing importation of Africans.

◎1650   ◎1700   ◎1750   1800◎

1661
Virginia passes law making Africans slaves for life.

1739
Stono uprising near Charleston, South Carolina.

1688
Quakers in Philadelphia formally protest slavery.

1790
Free African American population reaches 59,000.

GLOSSARY

ancestry • *(AN ses tree)* • Family members who lived long ago.

auction • *(AHK shun)* • Public sale at which each thing is sold to the person offering to pay the highest price.

bartered • *(BAHR tuhrd)* • To have paid for goods or services with other goods or services instead of with money.

black gold • *(BLAK GOHLD)* • A name given to Africans on the continent of Africa who were thought of as potential slaves.

bondage • *(BAHN dij)* • To be held or controlled completely by another person.

captives • *(KAP tivs)* • Persons caught and held prisoner, as in war.

Christians • *(KRIS chuns)* • People who believe in the religion based on the teachings of Jesus.

cultivation • *(kul tuh VAY shun)* • Preparation and use of land for growing crops.

debate • *(dee BAYT)* • To consider reasons for or against something.

discrimination • *(dis krim uh NAY shun)* • Unjust treatment based on race, religion, or sex.

economy • *(ee KAHN uh mee)* • System of producing, distributing, and using goods and services.

enslavement • *(in SLAYV mint)* • The act of being made to work for no wages or pay.

geography • *(jee AHG ruh fee)* • The natural features of a certain part of the earth.

griot • *(gree OH)* • An African storyteller who shares the history of Africa through stories.

heritage • *(HAR uh tij)* • A skill, right, or way of life handed down from a person's ancestors.

House of Burgesses • *(HOWS UHF BUR juhs es)* • The lower house of the legislature in colonial Virginia.

immigrants • *(IM uh grents)* • People who come to a foreign country, usually to settle there.

indentured servants • *(in DIN churd SUHR vants)* • Persons in colonial times who worked for someone for a specific amount of time in return for passage to the colonies.

indigo • *(IN du goh)* • A blue dye that comes from a certain plant of the pea family.

legislature • *(LEJ uh slay chuhr)* • A group of people who make laws.

midwives • *(MID weyevs)* • Women who take care of women during childbirth.

mutiny • *(MYOOT nee)* • A resisting or fighting against the leaders of a group. A rebellion on the sea.

overseers • *(OH vir see irs)* • People who supervised the work of slaves on plantations.

petitioned • *(peh TISH ind)* • To give a formal, written request, signed by a number of people, to someone in authority.

plantation • *(plan TAY shun)* • A large farm which mainly grows one crop.

population • *(pahp yoo LAY shun)* • The average number of people in a given area.

Puritans • *(PYOOR uh tuns)* • Persons who wanted freedom to worship their own way without separating from the Church of England.

Quakers • *(KWAYK urs)* • Members of a Christian religious group.

rebellion • *(rih BEL yun)* • An act of opposition to a governing group.

slave codes • *(SLAYV KOHDZ)* • Harsh laws designed to limit the activities of African slaves.

triangular trade • *(treye ANG yoo lur TRAYD)* • Trade routes that formed a triangle going toward and away from the American colonies or the West Indies.

uprisings • *(UP reyez ings)* • The act of rebelling or revolting.

Index ∿∿∿∿∿∿∿∿∿∿∿∿∿∿∿∿∿∿∿∿∿∿∿∿∿∿∿∿∿∿∿∿∿∿∿∿

A
Africa, 6-7, 15, 24, 30, 32, 34, 37, 39
African Heritage, 5, 14-15
Africans, 5-16, 18-26, 29-34, 36-41, 43 (See enslaved Africans, free Africans, and indentured servants.)
America 5-6, 8-9, 11, 16, 19, 21, 24, 34, 36, 41, 43
Angola (plantation), 11
Antoney, 7-9

B
black gold, 30

C
Catholics, 19
Christianity, 10, 14, 24, 31, 33
Congo, Simon, 23
Connecticut, 28, 41
cotton, 39

D
Delaware, 18, 26
discrimination, 10
Dutch, 7, 19, 23
Dutch West India Company, 22-23

E
England, 12, 24, 31
English, 5, 7, 11, 14, 30, 31, 39-40
enslaved Africans, 5-7, 9-14, 16, 18-26, 31-34, 36, 38-41, 43
    families, 13
    living conditions of, 12, 14, 16, 20, 33, 34
Equiano, Olaudah, 24
Escaped slaves, 37-38, 40-41
Estevanico, 9
Europeans, 5, 8-11, 19, 36, 38, 43

F
Florida, 40
free Africans, 6, 8-9, 11, 18, 20, 23-24, 26, 36, 38, 41

G
Georgia, 6
griot, 15

I
indentured servants, 8-11, 19-20, 22, 38
    terms of indenture, 8
indigo, 12, 39
Isabella, 7-9

J
Jamestown, 5-9
Jews, 19
Johnson, Anthoney and Mary, 11

L
Lay, Benjamin, 24-25

M
maps
    African American Population in Southern Colonies, 1750, 16
    English Colonies in 1750, 4
    Triangular Trade Routes, 30
    Tribes of West Africa, 32
Maryland, 6
Massachusetts, 28-29, 31
Middle colonies, 18-22, 26, 29

N
Native Americans, 9, 37-38, 40
New Amsterdam, 19, 23
New England colonies, 18, 28-34, 38, 43
New Hampshire, 28
New Jersey, 18
New Netherlands, 23
New York, 18-19, 22-24, 41

P
Pennsylvania, 18, 24, 26
plantations, 11-13, 14, 16, 19-20, 26, 43
Portuguese, Anthony, 23
Protestants, 19
Puritans, 31, 33

Q
Quakers, 19, 24-26

R
rebellions, 40-41
resistance, 5, 37-38, 40-41
Rhode Island, 28

S
skilled workers, 12, 21, 34
slave auction, 22
slave codes, 16, 33, 40
slavery, 5, 12-14, 18-19, 22-26, 31, 36 (See enslaved Africans, slave codes.)
slave trade, 7, 19, 28, 32 (See triangular trade.)
South Carolina, 6, 15
Southern colonies, 6, 8, 10-12, 14-16, 18-20, 26, 29, 40-41, 43
Spanish, 7, 9, 40
Stono Uprising, 40-41
sugar cane, 12

T
tobacco, 7-8, 12, 26, 39
triangular trade, 30

V
Virginia, 7, 16, 41

W
wheat, 21
Wheatley, Phillis, 29, 34
Williams, Peter, 20